For my sister and friend, Nancy Lowell George, with
thanks for your encouragement all along the way! And
for my family and friends, with much gratitude.
–S. L. G.

To my friends Melanie, Kristine, and Risa. Cheers to all
our adventures past and yet to come.
–J. W.

BEACH LANE BOOKS
An imprint of Simon & Schuster Children's Publishing Division • 1230 Avenue of the Americas, New York, New York 10020 • Text © 2021 by Sue Lowell Gallion • Illustration © 2021 by Joyce Wan • Book design by Karyn Lee © 2021 by Simon & Schuster, Inc. • All rights reserved, including the right of reproduction in whole or in part in any form. • BEACH LANE BOOKS and colophon are trademarks of Simon & Schuster, Inc. • For information about special discounts for bulk purchases, please contact Simon & Schuster Special Sales at 1-866-506-1949 or business@simonandschuster.com. • The Simon & Schuster Speakers Bureau can bring authors to your live event. For more information or to book an event, contact the Simon & Schuster Speakers Bureau at 1-866-248-3049 or visit our website at www.simonspeakers.com. • The text for this book was set in Baker Street. • The illustrations for this book were rendered digitally. • Manufactured in China • 0521 SCP • First Edition • 10 9 8 7 6 5 4 3 2 1 • Library of Congress Cataloging-in-Publication Data • Names: Gallion, Sue Lowell, author. | Wan, Joyce, illustrator. • Title: Pug & Pig and friends / Sue Lowell Gallion ; illustrated by Joyce Wan. • Other titles: Pug and Pig and friends • Description: First edition. | New York : Beach Lane Books, [2021] | Audience: Ages 0–8. | Audience: Grades K–1. | Summary: "Pug and Pig and their friends Robin and Squirrel love digging in the garden and zooming around the backyard together. But there's another "friend" in the backyard who isn't quite so friendly. That's Cat. What does Cat love doing? Cat loves sneaking up on Pug and scaring him! Pug does not think this is funny. And he does not like it at all. But when a thunderstorm comes and Cat gets scared up a tree, Pig, Robin, and Squirrel can't get her to climb down. Only Pug can help. But will he?"— Provided by publisher. • Identifiers: LCCN 2020052196 (print) | LCCN 2020052197 (ebook) | ISBN 9781534463004 (hardcover) | ISBN 9781534463011 (ebook) • Subjects: CYAC: Pug—Fiction. | Dogs—Fiction. | Pigs—Fiction. | Animals—Fiction. | Friendship—Fiction. | Play—Fiction. • Classification: LCC PZ7.1.G348 Po 2021 (print) | LCC PZ7.1.G348 (ebook) | DDC [E]—dc23 • LC record available at https://lccn.loc.gov/2020052196 • LC ebook record available at https://lccn.loc.gov/2020052197

PUG
& PIG

and Friends

written by
Sue Lowell Gallion

illustrated by
Joyce Wan

Beach Lane Books • New York London Toronto Sydney New Delhi

This is Pug and Pig's home.

These are Pug and
Pig's friends.

Pug, Pig, Squirrel, and Robin
like to explore in the bushes.

But not Cat.
She watches from the fence.

Pug, Pig, Squirrel, and Robin like to
zoom in circles around the yard.

But not Cat.
She watches from the porch.
What does Cat like to do?

Cat likes to surprise Pug.
Especially when Pug is
taking a nap.

MRROW!

arf!

Cat thinks this is funny.
So does Pig.
Pig loves surprises.

But Pug does not like surprises.

Neither do Squirrel or Robin.
They do not like surprises at all.

Now the sky grows dark.
Thunder rumbles.

Squirrel and Robin disappear
into their nests.

Pug and Pig disappear into their house.
What about Cat?

Crack! Lightning flashes.
Cat races high up into the tree.

Pug curls up on the front doormat.
He closes his eyes tight.
Is Pug taking a nap?

Cat watches Pug. Now Cat has an idea too.
Maybe Cat will climb down from the tree after all.

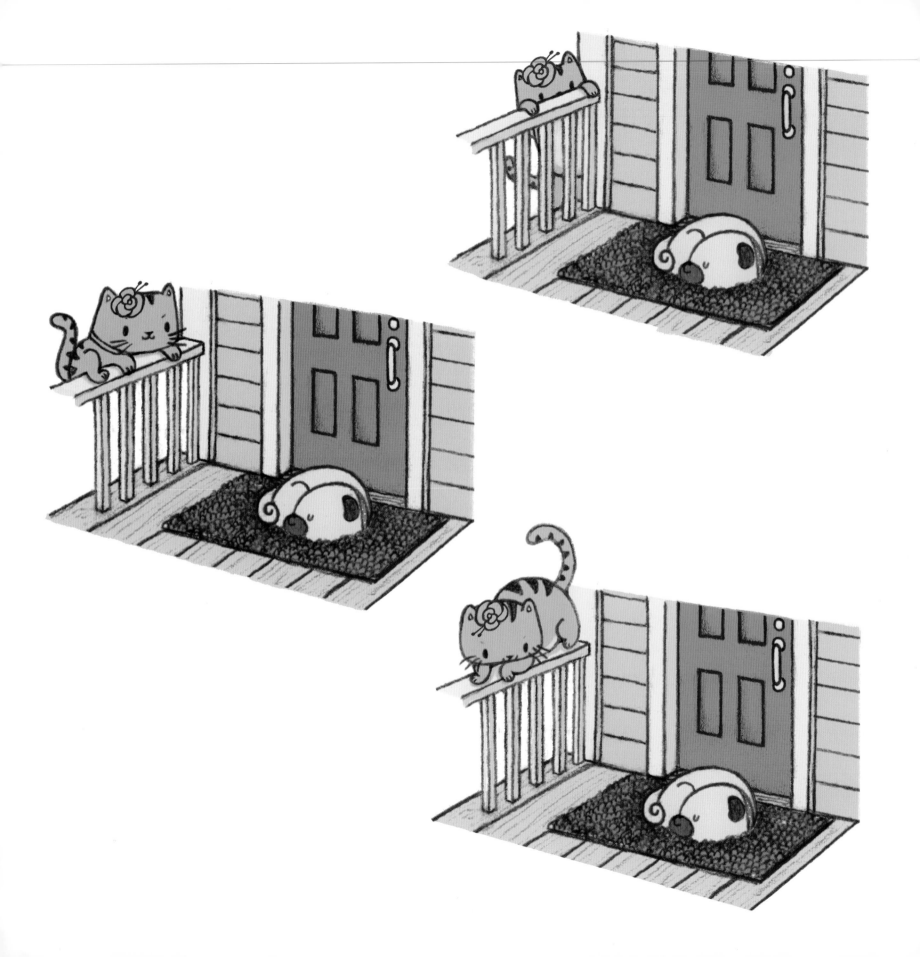

arf! arf! arf!

This time, the surprise is on Cat.

Pug thinks this is funny. Robin, Squirrel, and Pig think it is funny too.

And so does Cat!